F
Bra   Branscum, Robbie   c.1

The adventures of

Johnny May

The Adventures of Johnny May

The Adventures of
Johnny May

by Robbie Branscum

Illustrated by Deborah Howland

1 8 ⚐ 1 7
HARPER & ROW, PUBLISHERS
Cambridge, Philadelphia, San Francisco, London, Mexico City, São Paulo, Sydney
NEW YORK

THE ADVENTURES OF JOHNNY MAY
Text copyright © 1984 by Robbie Branscum
Illustrations copyright © 1984 by Deborah Howland
For information address Harper & Row Junior Books, 10 East 53rd Street, New York, N.Y. 10022. Published simultaneously in Canada by Fitzhenry & Whiteside Limited, Toronto.
Designed by Joyce Hopkins
2 3 4 5 6 7 8 9 10
FIRST EDITION

Library of Congress Cataloging in Publication Data
Branscum, Robbie.
    The adventures of Johnny May.

    Summary: As poor as any in the Arkansas hills,
Johnny May struggles against great odds to provide her
grandparents with a real Christmas.
    1. Children's stories, American. [1. Christmas—Fic-
tion.   2. Grandparents—Fiction.   3. Mountain life—
Fiction.   4. Arkansas—Fiction]   I. Howland, Deborah, ill.   II. Title.
PZ7.B73754Ad 1984   [Fic]   83-49464
ISBN 0-06-020614-4
ISBN 0-06-020615-2 (lib. bdg.)

Illustrations

One

I was clear to Huckleberry Hollow when I saw it. I mean, I knew there were lots of rotten logs in Huckleberry Hollow and that rabbits like to winter in old rotten logs.

I'd wrapped my feet in gunnysacks to keep the wet snow from seeping through my shoes, so I wasn't making any noise. The first thing I'd seen when I got to the Hollow was rabbit tracks, and later on people tracks.

Figuring that maybe Aron and his cousins were out hunting, too, I sort of hurried after the tracks. But when I got to the middle of the Hollow, nigh the bank of Big Creek where me and Aron fished in summer, I stopped. For through the trees came loud voices, men's voices. In fact, real mad-sounding men's voices.

I eased up to the screen of small saplings leaning under their weight of ice and peered through them. I saw Tom Satterfield facing Homer Ragland about twenty feet from me.

I heard Tom say, "Dad blame you to hell, Homer Ragland." He started to raise his gun, but before he could, Homer raised his. It seemed before my ears could take in the sound of the shot, Tom Satterfield was grabbing at himself and falling to the ground.

I was shocked, still as a mouse. I started to raise my own gun, thinking maybe I ought to shoot Homer Ragland, then decided that would be sort of silly since I didn't know why he'd shot Tom Satterfield. Besides, I didn't like Tom Satterfield anyways, because he was always loudmouthed and bragging.

On the other hand, it seemed a body ought not to be shot just because they were loud talking, because if they were, half of Arkansas would be killed deader than a doornail.

I stared at Homer Ragland, who was staring at Tom Satterfield like he didn't believe Tom was really laying so quiet in the snow.

I stared at Homer Ragland, who was staring at Tom.

Finally my senses came back to me, and I eased back slow and quiet until I was a long way toward home, then I ran, slipping and sliding, hurrying to get to Grandpa with what I'd seen. I ran out of breath below the hill to our house and had to stop to rest.

It was then the thought came to me. I mean the thought that I'd best keep my mouth *shut* about what I'd seen. With my face turning red, I remembered last year when I thought Mr. Berry had killed his wife, and told folks so, after reading my Bluebeard book. Hardly nobody liked Mr. Berry, but nobody believed he was a killer, like me and Aron had. And I knew for a fact that everybody in the hills liked Homer Ragland. So it stood to reason nobody would believe he shot anyone.

I mean, maybe Homer Ragland hadn't shot Tom Satterfield. Maybe he'd missed him, and Tom had fainted from being shot at. I mean, I would faint if somebody shot at me. Besides that, remembering all the trouble I had got me and Aron McCoy into, I figured I'd best be quiet.

When my breathing was easy, I walked slowly up the hill pondering. Last year when I heard Mr. Berry had four wives die on him, I figured it wasn't reasonable and thought he'd sent them on, himself. I really believed it and got Aron believing it, too, and I wound up making fools of both of us. Now Aunt Irene was wed to Mr. Berry and happy, it seemed, as a pig in a wallow.

Now if I went and told folks I'd seen Mr. Ragland shoot Tom Satterfield they'd say I was sure and certain crazy, bedbug crazy. I reckoned even Aron wouldn't believe me this time.

Of course, folks in the hills did get shot at and hit a lot, for there were still old feuds around. I mean, it wasn't an everyday thing, and lots of times it was years between shootings. It was a fact I'd never heard of Homer Ragland or Tom Satterfield feuding. But still, if a body couldn't believe their own eyes, what could they believe?

The only conclusion I came to before I reached the house was that I was going to keep my mouth shut until I heard something or Tom Satterfield's shot body was found. I stomped the snow off my feet and took the sacks off on the porch.

Grandpa and Grandma looked surprised at seeing me back so soon, so I hung the .22 over the fireplace, saying, "I couldn't see one durn rabbit track, Grandpa."

"You watch yer tongue, gal," Grandma snapped.

I muttered, "Sorry," and stuck my hands out to the flames of the fire.

It seemed strange to me that things could go from

bad to worse and still sort of stay the same. That's what I was thinking as I stared into the fire. I mean, I was still too fat, still dark eyed, and my hair was still red-brown, and turning eleven years old going on twelve hadn't made my freckles go away.

I gave a sigh that went plumb to my toes, thinking how for years I'd hated my old aunts and wished they'd go away, and now that they had, I wished they were back.

Irene had wed old Mr. Berry who lived on the bluff, and Irma finally married old Miz Hastings' boy Ivan— crossed eyes and all. When I begged her not to, she had said, "Now, Johnny May, yer old enough to keer for Ma and Pa."

But I wasn't, I told myself bitterly. For no matter how hard I figured, I couldn't figure any way of having a Christmas for them or me either, for that matter. And if I told myself the truth, it was me I was most worried about. I mean, Grandpa and Grandma had had a whole bunch of Christmases, and mine had been few and far between, what with Pa dying when I was real little and Ma going off and all.

Fact of the matter, nobody had heard from Ma for nigh on a year or more. Maybe the aunts were right, when they said she was no better than she had to be, I mean. Then again, that was always what hill women said about other hill women they didn't approve of.

I still had Aron McCoy, I told myself, knowing that was a dang lie. He wasn't mine, I just had him when he wanted me to. Oh, sometimes he'd hold my hand on the way to school, but he'd always drop it like a hot potato before the schoolhouse came in sight. He was scared silly that one of the boys would see him.

Sometimes I tried to hang on to him even when he was trying to shake me off. For I wanted fierce for the girls to see I had a feller. Aron wanted them not to see it was him just as fierce, though, and he flat wouldn't hold my hand in sight of the school.

There wasn't any school now, for the blue cold had taken hold of the Arkansas Hills, and as usual, the little one-room schoolhouse had closed its doors. But then the school shut down for almost any reason—planting time, harvesttime, and always in the winters. Most younguns had to walk so far to the school that they couldn't make it in the cold. I was glad; I had enough worry on my mind. I jumped when Grandpa said, "Wal, maybe 'tis too cold for even rabbits. Reckon pinto beans won't kill us fer a few more days."

"Looks to me like we ain't gonna have no rabbits, no beans, or no Christmas either," I said bitterly, glaring at the fire.

Grandma said, "Wal, youngun, there's allus a Christmas where there be anything or not."

"Wal, there won't be no presents or good food or nothin'," I said sourly.

"I shore cain't recall the Good Book a-sayin' that Christmas was presents and good food or such truck," Grandma said dryly. "Can you recall that, Pa?" Grandma and Grandpa always called each other Ma and Pa.

Grandpa pondered a mite, then spit a stream of tobacco juice in the can by the fireplace and said, "Naw, I cain't, Ma. Seems to me Christmas 'tis just the birthday of our Savior, Jesus, and come to think on it, He was birthed in a barn stall. Johnny May, Christmas 'tis to be thankful fer the Lord a-comin' to save us from our sins."

"Wal, I cain't help bein' more thankful iffen we had us a big ol' turkey gobbler and a heap of presents," I muttered, and headed for the kitchen before they could tell me how ungrateful I was.

I already knew it anyhow, that I was ungrateful, I mean. For I wanted Christmases like Sue Ella's, my town cousin's, with all the food and the presents. When Irma and Irene were home, they always filled my sock with an apple, an orange, a pack of store-bought chewing gum, and sometimes a big Baby Ruth candy bar. They made pies and cakes, too, and popped corn for the tree and strung red holly berries. We had a star, a big star, made from tin foil we'd saved.

Irma had cut the star from cardboard and we'd covered it with tin foil. It was real pretty at the very top of the tree, and when the flames from the fireplace flickered over it, it would shine just like a real star.

But Irene and Irma were gone. They'd be with their own families at Christmas. Besides, they were both in the birthin' way and wouldn't be apt to go out in the bad weather. So if there was to be a Christmas, I'd have to make it myself. I mean, I knew Christmas was because Jesus was born and came to earth to save us, and deep down I was real glad of it. Because there wasn't ever anybody needed saving worse than me. Of course, me and Aron both were saved last year at Revival time, but I seemed to let the cares of the world grab me by the tail and pull me in a downhill slide, and had to keep asking the Lord to forgive me. The Lord knew I had a temper that popped up when I least expected it. Of course He knew, too, that I was selfish, but that I really loved Grandpa and Grandma and wanted them a Christmas fierce, too, not just for myself.

I grabbed a leftover biscuit from the warming oven on the cookstove and, munching on it, went to the barn to shell more corn for the animals. Eyeing a fat speckled hen, I figured she would make good Christmas eating, but I knew Grandma wouldn't let me kill her. Sometimes in spring and summer, when the chickens were laying good, egg money was our only way of getting cash if the crops were bad.

The biscuit seemed to stick in my throat, and I felt sick as the corn kernels fell into the barrel at my feet. I tried not to think of Homer Ragland, and Tom Satterfield falling in the snow. The more I tried not to think of them, the more I did. I didn't remember seeing any blood, then reckoned maybe I hadn't stayed around long enough. I tried to think about what I knew about the men, but it didn't seem much. Maybe because I didn't pay too much mind to other folks because I thought on me most of the time.

I did know Homer Ragland lived over past Mr. Berry's place, and I did know that no matter what, I couldn't call Mr. Berry "uncle" though he'd married my aunt. I still couldn't like his red face and little bitty mean-looking blue eyes or the hair that grew out of his ears and nose.

Anyways, all I'd ever heard about Homer Ragland was good. I mean, what I could recall. I remembered Grandpa saying that Homer had a way with sick animals, real gentle, sort of like he and the animals understood each other. When anybody had an ailing mule, cow, or even a hound dog, Homer would come to care for them night or day. It seemed to me that a body that cared for hurtin' things that much wouldn't surely harm a human person.

Fact of the matter, Homer did look real gentle, sort of like a mule. I mean his face was long and he had big ears that stuck up on each side of his balding, dark head. He must be forty if he was a day, and Tom Satterfield was nigh twenty-five or -six, I reckoned. *He* was real good to look at, for an older person. He had flashing white teeth and bold, dark eyes. He was loudmouthed and boastful like, but all the big girls at pie suppers and revival meetings nigh fell over themselves to get near him.

I tried not to think on the men anymore, but it seemed the picture of what I'd seen wouldn't leave my head. Maybe I'll tell Aron. Just Aron.

Suddenly I made up my mind. Tomorrow I'd go rabbit hunting again, but the rabbits I'd hunt would be real close to Aron's house.

I stopped near the cellar and looked at our house like I'd never seen it before.

Our old house was the same as it had always been,

sitting above Big Creek. Except for wearing out a little more every year, it looked just like it had the year before, and the year before that. It perched high on its hill, the porch going all the way around, the four rooms inside it just the same, too.

Now that the aunts were gone, I had their bedroom for my own. The living room still had my small iron bedstead for when company came, and the old rockers Grandpa had made still sat in front of the rock fireplace.

We still used the kitchen most, with the big cast-iron cookstove and the oak table and benches. We had the same old heavy crock dishes, too, so old they were yellow with tiny cracks in them. Grandma said they had belonged to her ma's ma and she would never give them up. But I'd trade them in a minute for Miz McCoy's Blue Willow, so cheerful-looking on her sideboard. Of course we didn't have a sideboard, just an old washstand with a water bucket, washpan, and the old cracked mirror. One dang good thing—it was ours, all ours. I didn't let myself think maybe it was because nobody else wanted it.

I splashed water, ice-cold, on my face and hands, taking a quick swipe with the towel hanging on the nail, then rushed back inside to stand by the stove, watching Grandma take fresh butter from the churn, add salt, and beat the last drop of milk from it.

She took biscuits from the oven and called Grandpa, and as we sat down to eat, it seemed I really saw Grandpa and Grandma for the first time in a long time. I mean, really looked at them. Both of them were short and sort of fat, jolly-looking with their blue eyes and white hair. But Grandpa's hair was nigh gone and he moved real slow, because of rheumatism, he said. Made his joints pain, he said.

Grandma's face was nigh cracked as our old crock dishes. I felt a lump rise up in my gizzard and wondered again how the cat hair I was going to take care of them through this cold winter, let alone have them a Christmas, for it was already nigh December and the cold had come fast this year. So fast nobody was expecting it, and it had durn nigh froze all our onions and potatoes already.

Of course we had the stuff we'd canned from the summer truck garden, but it wouldn't last long if everything else froze and rotted.

The clouds hung heavy the next morning and spit small flakes of snow at my face as I made my way through the woods. I carried the .22 pointed at the ground away from me in case I slipped. But I didn't slow down to look for rabbit tracks. I was in a hurry to get to Aron McCoy's.

I wondered if his cousins were still with him, if their mother was still sick like Aunt Irene had said. I wondered, too, if they'd be stuck-up because they were from a town, like Sue Ella.

I wished I didn't think of Sue Ella so often, but she was and always had been like a thorn in my side. Even when she wasn't around, the thought of her made my lips taste sour. She made me feel fat! "Fact of the matter, ye are fat!" I muttered, and stomped on.

It was a long walk and I skirted around Huckleberry Hollow. I had a feeling I ought to keep my mouth shut about the shooting, even to Aron, but I felt I had to tell somebody or bust.

Two

All night long, every time I closed my eyes I'd seen Tom Satterfield grab himself and fall back in the snow. Maybe leastways Aron could go with me to see Tom's folks. I mean, to see if Tom had come home.

My nose felt nigh froze off by the time I got to Aron's place, but Miz McCoy made me feel right welcome, saying, "Why, Johnny May! What a nice surprise. Come in and get warm, child. Aron and his cousins are at the barn shelling grain for the stock."

Over her shoulder I could see Mr. McCoy sitting at the kitchen table reading to Aron's little brother and sister, for when there was no school he taught his younguns himself. Reckon Grandpa and Grandma would have taught me, too, 'cept they couldn't read as good as me. Fact was, I read them the Bible a lot because we didn't have any other books.

"I ain't real cold, Miz McCoy," I said, grinning at her, her so big and jolly-looking a body couldn't help smiling when she was around. "So I reckon I'll jest trudge on to the barn."

I was sorta disappointed because the cousins were still there. I'd wanted to talk to Aron alone. Besides, I liked it jest being me and Aron. I could hear laughing and talking before I got to the corncrib door, and a deep lonesome come over me for kinfolks of my own. I mean, friendly kind of kinfolks, not stuck-up like Sue Ella.

I opened the door to see two blond heads and a dark one bent over a grain barrel and stopped dead still, because three pairs of eyes were staring at me. The boy Scott looked enough like Aron to be his brother, except Aron had freckles and Scott didn't. His hair was gold colored like Aron's and his eyes blue as the sky after an April rain.

He smiled at me and my heart sort of flip-flopped, for his teeth were white and sparkly.

"Johnny May," Aron yelled, jumping up and grabbing my hand. He pulled me in the door, saying,

"These are my cousins, Scott and Bridgette, and this is Johnny May. I've been telling you about her," Aron said, smiling.

I turned to look at Bridgette and thought I'd never seen a girl so beautiful. No one I knew could hold a candle to her. Her hair was dark with copper streaks running through it and her eyes more amber than brown. She flashed a white smile at me real friendly like.

I said, "Howdy, Bridgette. Howdy, Scott."

They said, "Hi, Johnny May," and I could tell by their voices they were from a place where they had school most of the year round. They talked like Aron and his folks.

I leaned the .22 against the wall and sat down by the grain barrel with them, picking up an ear of corn to shell. Looking at me happily, Aron said, "What brought you out in this weather, Johnny May?"

"Got lonesome," I said into his blue eyes, but grinned at him with a look that said I had more to tell, but it was a secret.

He sort of nodded that he understood, then went on. "I had been wanting Scott and Bridgette to meet you, and Dad said he would drive us over Sunday if the road cleared enough. But if it didn't we were going to walk over anyway."

My heart felt nigh warm as my face. I mean, a good feeling just came all over me, because from those words I knew that Aron missed me as much as I did him.

Scott said, "Johnny May, is it true you were caught in a flood? Aron said you were and that you rode a log."

"Wal, reckon I did," I said, "but ridin' the log was mostly accident. I just sorta got hooked on it and hung on."

"I wish we lived here," Bridgette said wistfully. "Then Scott and I could hunt and fish with you and Aron. There's not all that much to do in town."

"Do ye hunt and fish?" I asked, surprised.

"Well, no." Bridgette laughed. "Aron has talked about it so much we feel like we do, though it'll take me a while to get used to picking up worms."

"Fishin' is fun," I said. "Sorta like a game between me and the fish. I mean, us sorta tryin' to outsmart each other. But I don't like huntin' much."

"Then why do you and Aron hunt so much?" Scott asked.

The picture of Grandpa and Grandma stripping the meat from tender young rabbits with toothless gums shot through my mind, and instead of answering I said, a little sourly, "There's shore a lot to do here, and I bet Aron didn't tell ye a body livin' here has to work like a mule."

"I wouldn't mind the work," Scott said, "as long as I got to hunt and fish, too. At least, I really want to try it before we go back home."

Every time Scott grinned, I thought lordy, lordy, if I'd have met him before I did Aron, I'd have liked him like I do Aron. Sort of sighing, I figured I'd stick with old Aron, though, freckles and all.

I bet if Sue Ella saw Scott, she'd bust a gut prancin' around in front of him. I already felt I might like Bridgette. I mean, she seemed so friendly, just so plain nice, a body could like her real easy.

"My cousin Sue Ella hates livin' on a farm," I said. "She lives in town and goes to movin' pitchers and ice-skatin' and stuff. They have electric lights and in-door toilets, and folks say we'll have sech in a few years." I sighed, then went on, "Be ye afeared of snakes and bugs, Bridgette?"

"Not unless they're the poisonous kind," she said, smiling.

"Sue Ella's scared of everything, leastways she lets on she is," I said hatefully.

"Oh, Sue Ella's all right," Aron said defensively, and I felt my ears turn red from jealousy. Then, re-membering Grandma saying that a body talking about a body looked worse than the body talked about, I said real fast, "Yep, she's just dandy." I said it real sweet, too, but I saw the gleam of laughing in Bridgette's eyes and knew she understood.

A good, soothin' sort of feeling rose up in me, because it was plainer every minute me and her might be friends. I decided I'd meet her halfway and said, "Maybe ye can come spend the night with me sometime, Bridgette," and she nodded.

Mr. McCoy came and stuck his head in the door and grinned, looking like an older Aron, saying, "You kids come and eat, Aron." And then, "Hi, Johnny May. You come and eat lunch with us, too."

I nodded and Aron said, "You guys go on. I want a word with Johnny May."

After they left, Aron looked at me square in the eye and said, "What's wrong, Johnny May? Is there trouble at your house?"

I shook my head and said, "Ain't no more trouble than usual at our house, Aron, but they's trouble right enough." And I told him what I'd seen while I was rabbit hunting yesterday. I wound up saying, "And I don't blame ye iffen ye don't believe me, Aron. I mean, since I made sech a durn fool of myself about Mr. Berry, I wouldn't blame ye a bit."

I hushed and stared at Aron. His face was sorta

white, and he said, "You been reading books again?"
I shook my head. "It's not that I don't believe you,
Johnny May. I've never known you to lie, except for
a good reason. It's just hard for me to believe such a
gentle, kind person as Homer Ragland would hurt
anything, let alone a human."

"I know, Aron. I seen it and I still cain't believe it.
I mean, I ain't told nobody but you 'cause I don't want
Mr. Ragland to be put in jail or nothin' 'til I know
for shore."

"You are right about that, Johnny May. Listen,"
Aron said, his eyes starting to glitter like when he got
excited about something, "Scott and Bridgette and I
were going to pick out our Christmas tree after lunch.
Instead we'll go with you to Huckleberry Hollow and
see if we can find the body or some clues. Okay?"

Grinning a sigh of relief, I said, "Okay." Then, "Are
ye shore it's safe to tell yer cousins? I mean, can they
keep a secret?"

"Oh, sure. We've had a lot of secrets between us,"
Aron said. "As a matter of fact, when we lived close
together, we did a lot of secret things."

"Wal, I reckon four heads is better than one," I
said, "so let's go eat so's we can be on our way. I got
to be home afore dark."

Miz McCoy's table was piled high with food, and

not a pinto bean in sight. I noticed Scott and Bridgette ate almost as much as me and Aron. It kept Miz McCoy hopping to put more biscuits on the table. Later me and Bridgette cleaned up the dishes real fast. Scott and Aron even helped.

Pulling on his coat, Aron said, "Dad, it might be late when we get back. We're going to walk Johnny May home and look for a Christmas tree to cut later."

"All right," Mr. McCoy called.

"Come see us again real soon, Johnny May." Miz McCoy smiled at me, and I grinned back.

Aron carried the .22 for me, and as we walked toward Huckleberry Hollow he told Bridgette and Scott about the murder I thought I'd seen. Their mouths dropped open and Scott said, "We'd better call the cops."

Aron laughed and explained, "There are no cops in these hills. Just an old fat sheriff in town. And besides, me and Johnny May don't want to get Homer Ragland in trouble. He's a very nice man, and he may not have killed Tom Satterfield at all."

"Then we'd better tell your dad, Aron," Bridgette said quietly.

"No!" I snapped, looking Scott and Bridgette in the eyes. "We cain't tell nobody. I don't want to feel like a fool agin less I have to. 'Sides, we wouldn't have told ye, if we thought ye were going to tell."

For a moment they looked uncertain, then they nodded and promised not to tell any grown-ups until me or Aron said so.

We were all quiet when we got to Huckleberry Hollow, for when we'd pushed through the saplings where I'd seen Homer and Tom, there on the snow, plain as could be, was blood. When the spitting snow from the sky fell on it, it was soaked up and turned red, too. There was no body, just blood, frozen blood, nigh cold as my own was turning.

There was no body, just blood, frozen blood.

Three

"Well, Scott, it sure looks like Johnny May is right," Aron said, bending over the bloody spot, peering at it.

"But there's no body, Aron," Scott said, looking around like one might pop out from behind a tree.

"Be careful where you guys step," Bridgette said, "and we might be able to see some clues, I mean footprints or something."

"Then we best hurry," I said, " 'cause the way the snow's coming down, all signs will be covered up by it soon."

We all rose up and stood still, our eyes searching the ground. Suddenly Scott whispered, "Hey, look, you guys. Something's been dragged that way, toward the creek bank."

We followed his pointing finger and saw a deep, wide groove in the snow, and it led straight to the creek.

Slowly and carefully we followed the groove to the bank. There, filling up fast, was one set of footprints going away from the creek. They were going toward Homer Ragland's place.

We stopped and just sort of stared at each other. I broke the silence, saying, "Oh cat hair, Aron! What're we gonna do now? You know how everybody likes Homer Ragland. They'd never believe he killed a body."

I thought about Homer's big brown eyes, as gentle as one of the cows he doctored.

"I know, Johnny May," Aron said seriously. "Not long ago he cured our horse of colic, and Mom and Dad think he's just about the nicest person around."

"So does Grandpa and Grandma and the rest of the Arkansas Hills," I said thoughtfully.

"What are you going to do?" Scott and Bridgette asked in almost the same breath. "Call the sheriff now?" Me and Aron looked at each other, and I knew we were both remembering how wrong I'd been about thinking Mr. Berry was a killer.

"Hey, Aron, I really think you ought to either call

whatever law there is around here or let your dad decide what to do," Scott said.

Finally Aron spoke. "I think we'd best all just keep our mouths shut and try to find out what we can on our own. I mean, I don't think anyone would believe us. And besides, by the time we get back here with Dad or anyone else, the snow would have all traces covered, anyway.

"Besides that," he went on, "we have the excuse of finding our Christmas tree, and we can drag out looking for it quite a while."

Turning to me, he asked, "You found your tree yet, Johnny May?" I shook my head, not telling him I doubted we'd have a Christmas this year.

"Well then, we can go out 'most every day looking for a tree. It'll be a couple of weeks before time to cut them, anyway," Aron said, "and we can meet Johnny May here and go nose around Homer Ragland's and Tom Satterfield's places some and see what we can find out."

"Boy, Aron, yer shore smart a-thinkin' that up real quick," I said admiringly, and Scott, his blue eyes lit up, nodded.

Bridgette looked a little worried as she said, "If this man you're talking about did kill Mr. Satterfield, do you think he might try and kill us, too?"

"Naw," Aron shook his head. "He won't know that we know, y'see."

Bridgette nodded her dark head and Scott said, "Oh boy! Just like a movie, eh, Bridgette?" and they both laughed when he added, "Only better, because we're in it."

We all knew is wasn't really funny, for everybody liked—or more like, loved—Homer Ragland.

"You know, Aron," I said, "even if Tom Satterfield was tossed in the creek, we couldn't find him now. 'Cause look how fast the water's freezing."

We all looked at the ice coating the water, and Aron nodded his head, saying, "You're right, Johnny May. If it stays this cold, by tomorrow Big Creek will be one chunk of ice, and not even a fish, let alone a human, can be seen under the ice, so we'd better see what we can now."

I nodded and eyed the narrow crick bank on both sides as I walked up and down, with Aron, Scott, and Bridgette following suit. But there was nothing to be seen except the snow starting to coat the ice already forming on the water.

"Wal, I cain't look no more now. I got to try and find some rabbits to kill," I said. "I been tellin' Grandpa and Grandma for two days that I'd get them some

28

rabbits. They ain't got no teeth, ye know," I explained to Scott and Bridgette, "so's I have to try and find young ones."

"We'll help you," Aron said, and I nigh laughed, remembering that last year Aron thought even killing a chicken was murder. Of course, he was new to the hills then.

For the rest of the day me and Aron showed Scott and Bridgette how to find rabbit tracks and follow them to hollow logs. We showed them how to cut forked sticks from trees with their pocketknives and how to poke the sticks into the hollow logs and twist the rabbits out with the sticks.

When we finally found some good rabbit logs, Bridgette jabbed her forked stick in one and sort of scared some rabbits out by accident. Aron knocked them on the head with a bigger stick he'd found, saying there was no use wasting bullets. Blood from the rabbits' heads sprinkled the snow and turned it a bright red as their gray-and-white bodies went limp and their eyes dulled over.

I heard a gasp, and turned to find Bridgette leaning against a tree, her face white like she was going to faint. Scott was sorta hanging on to her, not looking so good himself.

"Poor little rabbits," Bridgette whispered, and for a moment I saw me and Aron through her eyes—the blood on our hands and clothes—and I knew there must have been a hungry, eager look on my face. I felt half sick too, now, my belly turned, and I said harsh like, "Some folks cain't go to the store, ye know, and I bet ye don't run down a meat counter saying 'pore li'l steak,' or 'pore li'l pork chops,' do ye?"

Aron nigh made me swallow my tongue, 'cause he said real quiet, "It's different on a farm, you guys, and here in the hills some people wouldn't have meat at all if they couldn't hunt." He means folks like me, I thought, feeling hot with shamed pride.

"We aren't saying it's wrong, Johnny May," Scott said. "It's just that we never saw anything killed before, and I guess it was sort of a shock."

"I never thought about it before—that something had to die before we ate it," Bridgette said in a soft little voice, and I felt my belly turn over again and wondered if I could ever kill again. But the picture of Grandma and Grandpa flashed in my head, and I knew I could. Whether I could eat what I killed was something else again, and I said 'most gentle, "Ye'll like fishin'," and for lack of a better way to explain it, I added, "It's clean."

Still, for Grandma and Grandpa's sake I was proud of the five rabbits. There were three young ones, and two were sort of old, but Grandma could stew them a long time.

It was getting late, so we said a quick "See ye tomorrow," and I nigh ran home, knowing I had a heap of chores to do before I'd be free to Christmas tree hunt. I mean, for Grandpa and Grandma to *think* I was Christmas tree hunting.

They were real proud of the rabbits. Grandpa said, "I swan, Johnny May, these here rabbits will feed us fer days."

"They's fat, too," Grandma said, honing a knife to clean them.

I hung the .22 over the fireplace saying, "Wal, Aron and his cousins helped with catchin' 'em. I run into them out in the woods and they wont to know iffen I can Christmas tree hunt with them fer a few days. Can I, Grandpa, iffen I keep all the chores done?"

"Wal, I reckon, youngun," Grandpa said. And Grandma added, "It takes a right smart spell fer a body to find a tree jest right. Oncet yer aunts took nigh on two months afore findin' one that suited them both."

Grandma gave a deep sigh, and I knew she missed Irma and Irene fierce, them being her youngest and all. I knew Grandpa hated not being able to get out in the cold to do the chores, too. But he did all he could.

I didn't blame Grandpa and Grandma for anything, for cross-eyed weasels could see they'd raised me best as they could. If there was ever any trouble, it was almost all caused by me.

I hated being poor, but truth to tell, I hated being poor a lot for Grandpa and Grandma's sake, too. While I raked out the barn stalls and pitched clean hay down from the barn loft, I daydreamed of being rich, real rich, maybe even having five hundred or a thousand dollars.

I'd buy Grandpa and Grandma new teeth for Christmas, some bright linoleum for the floor like Sue Ella's mom had in town, and I'd buy a car and learn how to drive it. No, I'd buy a truck—that way we could haul our own crops to town and sell them. I'd get us another fattening hog, maybe two. I'd get yard goods for me and Grandma, bright, cheerful dresses. I'd get Blue Willow dishes. I'd get me a store-bought fishing pole, too, like Aron and his pa had. I'd get padded chairs for Grandpa and Grandma, and a radio so we could hear Amos 'n' Andy—of course, it'd have to be a battery one, because of us not having electricity, but boy would our feet tap on Saturday nights when the Grand Ole Opry was on.

I fed the animals, milked the cow, giving the barn cat some of the milk, and dreamed on 'til dark came and Grandma yelled, "Come to supper, Johnny May."

Remembering the rabbits, I almost ran and, since Grandma wasn't looking, just sort of wiped my hands at the washstand. I couldn't hardly wait until Grandpa said thank you to the Lord.

Grandma had fried the young rabbits and made biscuits and milk gravy to go with them. On top of that, she'd opened a can of tomato preserves. I let Grandma and Grandpa stuff, and held myself to beans and tomato preserves, though it was hard, with the smell of the rabbit teasing my nose.

Grandma said, "Ye ailing, gal? Ye ain't eatin' no rabbit."

"Reckon I ate too much at Aron's house, Grandma," I said, rubbing my belly. "I just got plumb overfull."

"Wal, I do reckon there's a first time for ever'thing," Grandpa laughed, and Grandma smiled with him.

I smiled, too, to watch them enjoy the rabbits and know it was me that provided them. Truth to tell, I think I enjoyed watching them eat even more than they enjoyed the eating.

Four

Miz Ragland opened the door to our knock, saying, "Why, Johnny May and Aron McCoy, what're y'all a-doin' out in this here weather?"

"Lookin' fer our Christmas tree," I said real fast. Aron introduced Bridgette and Scott to her.

Miz Ragland had real big blue eyes and corn-colored hair braided and wrapped around her head. She was real friendly, just like Homer. I felt sort of bad, I mean her asking us in and all, and us being here to find out if her man was a killer. Besides that, it was plain to see Miz Ragland was in the birthin' way, and before very long by the looks of her belly.

When I came out of my thoughts, Aron was saying, "We thought since Mr. Ragland goes around the woods so much helpin' folks, we thought we might ask him if he'd spotted any really nice Christmas trees."

"Wal, he's in the barn doctoring one of the cows. You all jest go on out there and ask him." Saying "Thank you" and "Y'all come," we headed for the barn. I hadn't been just mouthing words—I really hoped Miz Ragland would come and visit Grandma.

It was a big barn painted red. Fact was, Homer Ragland's barn was almost nicer than our house. Reckon it was because he liked the animals so much. Inside the big double doors of the barn it even smelled good. Like milk and sun trapped in the clean, fresh straw that covered the floors of the stalls. It smelled of a newborn calf, still wet and curly from its ma's tongue bath.

Homer was wiping down the cow, saying real gentle, "Yer jest fine, Bessie. Ye done a right fine job." He looked up and saw us, his large, dark eyes as gentle and soft as the eyes of the cow he was rubbing with a cloth.

He smiled, saying, "Why howdy, younguns. Ye got some new folks there with ye, ain't ye, Aron?"

Aron explained about Bridgette and Scott being

35

cousins come to stay for the winter, then added, "We just stopped by thinking maybe you'd know where the best Christmas trees are."

Homer rubbed his balding head thoughtfully and said, "Wal, I reckon the best to be found is over nigh the old Turner place. Got some real nice fat cedar and pine both."

We sort of stood on one foot and then the other for a spell, not knowing what else to say, and knowing durn well we couldn't just up and ask, "Did you kill Tom Satterfield?" So I said, "Wal, thank you. Reckon we best be on our way."

When we were out of sight of the house, Scott said, "I can't believe a man that kind to animals could shoot another human being. I still think we should at least tell your dad, Aron," he added a little stiffly. "I mean, I just can't believe one person can kill another so easily."

"I couldn't either if I hadn't seen the blood," Aron said. Then, reaching out to take my hand, he went on, "And I know Johnny May wouldn't lie to me."

"I don't blame ye none, Scott," I said, "fer a-doubtin', 'cause I done seen the shootin' myself and I don't hardly believe it."

"If Mr. Ragland did shoot Mr. Satterfield, he must

36

have had a good reason," Bridgette said thoughtfully. The rest of us nodded agreement.

Then she said, "I think we should tell your dad, too, Aron."

Aron looked at my hand like he was surprised he was really holding it, then dropped it, saying, "No, we won't tell him, at least not yet."

"I can see you wanting to wait, Aron," Scott said softly, his blue eyes serious. "Mr. Ragland is such a kind man."

"I never did hear nothin' good about Tom Satterfield, have you, Aron?" I asked.

He thought for a moment, then said, "I haven't heard much about him at all, except for Dad saying once that Tom was mostly a boasting, bragging mouth."

"I heerd Grandpa say he thought Tom run bootleg whiskey," I said.

Then, stopping under a tall pine, its branches hanging heavy with snow, Aron said, "Well, it's not far from here to the Satterfield place. We could stop by with the same excuse as we used at the Raglands'. Maybe we could find out if Tom is missing or something."

"Wal, let's hurry," I said, " 'cause I wont to stop by

and see Irene on the way back. Grandma will be right glad to hear how she's gettin' on."

"I hope Mr. Berry's not there," Aron said firmly, and I agreed.

"Why don't you guys like Mr. Berry?" Scott asked.

I held my breath, hoping Aron wouldn't tell his cousins what a fool I'd made of myself over Mr. Berry, then let it out with a whoosh when Aron only said, "Oh, Mr. Berry's sort of a creep," and let it go at that.

The Satterfield place was so rundown it made our house look real good. The yard fence sagged to the ground here and there, and the gate had plumb fallen off. The porch steps and the porch itself had missing boards and we had to trod carefully to the door.

Old Miz Satterfield, Tom's ma, come to the door, and she wasn't friendly at all. Her little eyes glared at us suspicious like as she wiped her hands on a greasy apron, saying in a harsh voice, "What ye younguns want?"

"We want to know if you and your boy Tom know where we can find good Christmas trees," Aron said real fast.

Miz Satterfield's little gray eyes glittered, her nose nigh touching her chin over a toothless mouth, and she snapped, "Ye better not be a-cuttin' no trees offen our land. Now git, ye hear me!"

She slammed the door in our faces and we got, fast, until we were out of sight of the house. Then Scott grinned. "Man, that old woman is mean."

"Maybe she's just tired," Bridgette said kindly, and I sort of nodded, thinking maybe she was right. Aron looked thoughtful, but said nothing as we plodded on through the snow.

"I wish we knowed if we was lookin' fer a dead body, er jest one walkin' around shot," I said.

Aron said, "We'll just have to think of a way to ask around about Tom Satterfield without anyone knowing why we're asking. Sooner or later someone is bound to realize they haven't seen him in a while. I mean, his mother is not about to let us inside the house."

We nodded agreement and I said, "You all c'mon. We best hurry, 'cause I've got chores to do 'fore dark."

We hurried as fast as the snow and ice would let us to Mr. Berry's place on the bluff. Because the ladder to the bluff was gone, we had to go the long way around. Scott and Bridgette thought it was really neat living on a bluff looking out over Big Creek, and said so over and over. Me and Aron didn't say any-

"Now git, ye hear me!"

thing. Reckon we were too worried Mr. Berry would be home, and he was.

It was him who opened the door, and his little blue eyes and red face looked sour when he saw us. But he didn't say anything, for Irene came flying, hugging me and saying how proud she was to see us. She made Scott and Bridgette welcome and insisted we eat some dinner with them.

"How's Ma? How's Pa?" she asked, hugging me again. "I'm so glad ye come, why don't ye come more?" I couldn't hardly tell her that if we did her husband would no doubt throw rocks at us. Nor did I tell her we was not apt to have a Christmas with her gone.

Irene's belly was big in the birthin' way, same as Miz Ragland's. She looked real happy, and I figured she surely knew something good about Mr. Berry that I didn't.

She took real good care of his house, for it was shining clean, and the little younguns by one of his wives seemed to look on Irene as their ma. She laughed and talked to them as they helped her set the table.

Me and Aron kept a wary eye on Mr. Berry while we stuffed ourselves on corn bread, green beans, and ham hocks. It wouldn't have surprised either of us if he'd stood up and suddenly yelled for us to get away from his table, but he didn't.

He went to the barn as soon as he'd finished eating, with a fast nod to us, and I was glad he did. Irene packed a basket of food for me to take home to Grandma and Grandpa.

Feeling full and warm, we started to walk home, and at the bridge that crossed Big Creek we promised to meet the next day.

Instead of going straight to the house, I went around it to the barn, carrying the heavy basket. I wanted to see what Irene had sent. I mean, if there was something that would keep, I'd hide it 'til Christmas so we could have something good then. Maybe if I'd be like a squirrel, I told myself, we'd have a Christmas after all. I mean, sort of hiding bits and pieces of things.

I stopped to lean against the barn door, feeling all mixed up and alone like I'd never felt alone before, even though Bridgette had showed plain she'd like to be my friend. But I didn't see how I could be a friend to nobody 'less my insides got well. They was all sick feeling, had been since I'd seen Homer Ragland shoot Tom Satterfield, and somehow killing rabbits had got all mixed up with it, too. I mean, maybe nobody had a right to kill nothin' else.

The worry of Grandpa and Grandma came over me again, but I didn't cry. What good would it do?

Five

I scrooched down in the barn stall and opened the basket. There were two raisin pies that smelled so good I could have eaten one by myself, but I knew we'd have them for supper. There was a large jar of pear preserves that would keep for Christmas and a jar of small green tomato pickles. I took both jars and hid them deep in the sawdust of the empty apple barrel in the corncrib. That way they wouldn't freeze. I put the raisin pies back in the basket along with the loaf of pumpkin bread Irene had sent.

I took the basket to Grandma and rushed to do the chores. Later, while we ate a supper of boiled rabbit and fluffy dumplings, I told Grandpa and Grandma about our visit to Irene, making it sound a lot nicer than it was. I mean, I just sort of made it sound like Mr. Berry was a mite overcome with joy at seeing us at his table. I thought I might have gone plumb crazy, for the rabbits surely tasted good, but I made myself not think on it too much, about the killing of them, I mean.

I told them we hadn't found a tree that suited us for marking for the Christmas cutting and planned on looking 'til we did. I said how nice and friendly Aron's cousins were, and that maybe me and Bridgette could write each other when she went home, maybe be pen pals only better, 'cause we'd met already.

"Friends is a really nice thing to have, Johnny May," Grandma said, wiping suds from her hands.

Thinking about friends, I once more thought of Homer Ragland, and how Tom Satterfield must have done something real bad to get a good, gentle man like Homer to shoot him.

We just got the dishes done when Grandma said, "Oh, Johnny May, I 'most forgot. They was a postcard in our box today a-sayin' Sue Ella won't be able to come fer Christmas. Ain't that a shame?"

"Shore is, Grandma," I muttered, thinking it was the best news I'd heard in I don't know when.

When we were sitting in front of the fireplace, I said, "Grandpa, we went by Miz Satterfield's place today to see iffen they was any nice Christmas trees around their place, and she was real unfriendly. How come, ye reckon?"

But it was Grandma who answered me, sort of shaking her head and saying, "Poor Morlee—that's Miz Satterfield's name, Johnny May. Me and her was girls together and, poor thing, she wed a bad'un, she did. She did do that. Her man was a whiskey-makin', bootleggin' braggart who drank more than he sold, I reckon. Plumb mean, he was. Bad to beat on Morlee and the younguns, and was in the state pen more than oncet, I reckon. He died in the pen, stabbed by somebody. Folks never found out who done it and I reckon Morlee's boy, Tom, took after his pa, from what I hear. Ye jest overlook Morlee's unfriendliness, Johnny May. She's had her a load to carry, she do."

I nodded my head and said nothing more, but listened real close when Grandpa said, "Wal, that boy Tom is a-headin' fer trouble. I heerd Sheriff Treat was after him jest a week or so ago for some meanness or the other."

I went to bed thinking about Tom, and I thought if Homer had tossed him in the creek he wouldn't be found 'til spring thaw, thick as the ice was freezing on that water.

Then I thought about Bridgette and me, and how she wasn't uppity and wore britches just like I did, and her every bit as pretty as Sue Ella.

December was a week old now, and it seemed to me Christmas was flying fast right at me. I decided to take the .22 when I went to meet Aron and his cousins, in case we did come on something to eat. Even a possum would be good, I figured, almost any kind of meat would stay froze in this kind of weather 'til Christmas. I had to do it for Grandpa and Grandma, I told myself fiercely.

Of course, we had a few pumpkins in the barn, but who the cat hair ever heard of folks just having pumpkin pie for Christmas and nothing else? And a Christmas tree with nothing under it?

"Your face looks like it's gonna plumb cloud up and rain, Johnny May," Grandpa said. "Somethin' ailin' ye, gal?"

"Naw," I said, raising my head to smile at him. "I was jest thinkin' on the best place to hunt rabbits, Grandpa. I reckoned I might as well hunt rabbits and Christmas trees both."

"Wal, iffen a rabbit seen you lookin' that fierce, ye

wouldn't need no gun, he'd jest nachurly fall over," Grandpa cackled, and Grandma laughed, too.

I ate another biscuit and headed for the barn to get the chores done. Clouds still hung heavy, but the snow had stopped spitting and it was a cold, crisp kind of weather where everything crackled and crunched underfoot. The ice-coated trees tinkled overhead like glass chimes.

I did the chores in no time flat and gave the barn cats more warm milk than usual, figuring the mice they were supposed to live on and keep from the corncrib were no doubt frozen to death. I wrapped my feet in gunnysacks, tying the sacks on with heavy string. Grabbing the .22 and filling my pockets with shells, I was at the bridge by sunup.

Aron, Bridgette, and Scott were already there, stomping their feet and whopping their hands together to keep warm. Of course, they all had gloves and rubber boots, but I reckoned in this weather even fur coats wouldn't keep a body warm.

"What did you bring your gun for, Johnny May? Going to shoot your Christmas tree?" Aron laughed.

"Oh, I thought I might happen on some rabbits or somethin'," I said, like it didn't matter one way or the other.

"You know, Dad saw a deer over by the old sink-hole the other day," Aron said, and before I thought, I said, "Boy, I bet a deer would make good Christmas eatin'."

Scott said, "Don't you like turkey, Johnny May?"

"Oh, sure," I said, unconcerned as I could, "but venison is good fer a change."

"We're going to have a big fat goose," Aron said. "Every year Mom picks the biggest goose we have. She puts it in a pen and gets it real fat, and yum, yum." Aron grinned, rubbing his belly. For a moment I 'most hated Aron and his durn goose. I 'most hated anybody who had folks to worry about their food and their Christmas.

"We've always had turkey," Bridgette said. "Mom buys them at the grocery store."

"How is yer ma?" I asked before one of them could ask me what we were having for Christmas.

"She's doing well," Scott said. "She hurt her back in a car wreck and had to have it operated on. Dad wrote that by the first of the year she'll be walking good again."

"Well, that's real good news," I said, then added, "But I reckon right now we best get a-lookin' fer Tom Satterfield's body—though if it's really froze in the crick under all that ice, we won't see it."

As we walked back toward where I'd seen the shooting, I told them what Grandpa and Grandma had told me about the Satterfield family, and added casually as I could, "Oh, Aron, we got a postcard saying Sue Ella can't come fer Christmas this year."

"Is that Johnny May's cousin, the one you said was so pretty, Aron?" Scott asked.

I felt my ears start to turn red, but Aron said, calmly, "Yep, but you can't take her rabbit hunting or anything like that. She's really scared of bugs and snakes, and almost everything."

Bridgette gave me a look that said, "Uh-huh," and I knew she knew what I was feeling. There wasn't anything on this earth I knew of that Sue Ella was really afraid of, 'less it was not catching the eye of a boy she liked.

"I wouldn't mind taking care of her," Scott grinned. Aron shot him a dirty look, and I needed a rock to chew on again. For it was plain to see old Aron could be jealous of Scott and Sue Ella, though he claimed to like me best.

I pushed on ahead, thinking maybe I'd go over by the old sinkhole tomorrow and see if I could find any sign of the deer Aron's pa had seen. Soon we came to the spot where I'd seen Homer Ragland shoot Tom Satterfield. We stared down at the ground. Sure enough, the snow of two days before had covered every sign, and where there had been a pool of blood, now it was pure white.

We went to the crick bank, but couldn't see through the ice, which was thick by now. We hadn't really expected to see anything, I told myself, so it was plumb silly the way we were all standing around real hushed and quiet . . . as if death was all around us in the still woods.

Six

Out of the blue, Scott said, "It's not possible for a person to murder someone and not anyone know, is it?"

"Well, *we* know," Aron said. "The thing is, we can't prove it. Johnny May saw the shooting and we saw the blood, but I doubt anyone in the hills would believe us if we said anything."

"Well, even if they did believe us, Aron, they wouldn't let on," I said. "I mean, folks jest keer too much fer Homer Ragland to cause him grief. And reckon they ain't nobody here who ain't wonted to kill Tom Satterfield at one time or the other."

51

"Then why are we looking for a body, if no one cares?" Bridgette asked.

"Well, I reckon his ma does," I said.

Then Aron, his blue eyes looking serious, said, "Besides that, Bridgette, people just can't *kill* other people, even if they are real nice like Homer Ragland."

"It shore beats the cat hair outa me what to do now," I said.

Scott spoke up, saying, "We could find out where Tom Satterfield hung around the most and ask people if they'd seen him."

"Whar Tom hung out wouldn't let us in," I said, " 'cause I heerd someplace he allus hung out in pool halls and sech in town. 'Sides, we ain't got no way to go to town."

"Anyway, we can't stay and look today, Johnny May," Aron said. "Dad wants us to shell the corn for the stock, and the barn has to be cleaned. We'll be by to get you tomorrow, and we'll search for Tom some more or go see Homer Ragland and see if he's looking bad or something."

I nodded and waved as they left, figuring I could go to the old sinkhole and try and find the deer today. My feet felt frozen as I waded the snow toward the old sinkhole, and my nose was numb, and come to think on it my ears and fingers, too, but I kept going.

The sinkhole was a good fifty feet wide and least-ways seventy-five or a hundred feet deep. I stood on the edge and stared down at it thinking it would be a good place to hide a body. But I couldn't see nothing but snow at the bottom; then looking around me I saw the deer tracks leading to the stretch of timber above the sinkhole, and I followed them.

When I reached the timber, I crept quietly after the tracks, and not far into the woods I looked up and saw the deer, staring at me over the top of a rotten log covered with ice and snow.

I raised the .22 slowly so as not to startle the young buck standing there. Then just as slowly I lowered the gun, for the deer's eyes were large and brown, sort of like Irene's and Irma's, and truth to tell, mine, too. I couldn't kill something so alive. I mean not ever, even for Grandpa and Grandma's Christmas.

"You jest git outa here," I hollered at it. "Don't you know you could git yerself killed? You git to tall timber, you hear?" And I watched as it turned and leaped gracefully over fallen logs, rocks, and branches, its head held proud.

Then I turned toward home. My shoulders felt weighted down with worry, and the gun almost too heavy to carry. I cussed myself, knowing how much the deer meat would have meant to us, but when I recalled the big dark eyes, real gentle eyes, staring at me, I was glad I hadn't pulled the trigger. I'd just have to think up some other way to get us a Christmas feast.

Tears of self-pity ran down my cheeks, and my face was so cold they felt scalding hot. I felt lost in a white, cold world that I didn't know anymore.

"Blast them ol' aunts to blazes, anyway," I muttered out loud. "All they keered about was a-featherin' their own nests and a-leavin' me to keer fer Grandma and Grandpa by m'self. And a piss-pore job ye're doin' of it, too, Johnny May," I hissed, and I knew if I had that deer in my gunsight right then I would've shot it.

Then the thought crossed my mind that maybe that's why Homer Ragland shot Tom Satterfield. Not to eat, I mean, but because he felt desperate, like me.

The tears were freezing to ice on my face, and I swiped them off with Grandpa's old coat sleeve and hurried fast as I could toward home. My feet were so cold I couldn't feel them anymore, and my hands so numb I carried the gun under my arm.

By the time I stumbled up on the porch, Grandma had the door open, saying, "Lord have mercy! Pa! Pa, come and hep me with this youngun. She's nigh froze."

They pulled me in, taking the gun, and half dragged me to the fireplace, rubbing my hands and feet. Grandma started pouring hot sassafras tea down me.

When the feeling came back to my body, Grandpa said, "Whar you been, youngun? You know better than to stay out 'til ye're froze board stiff."

"I was trackin' a deer," I mumbled, and told him about Aron and his cousins having to go home, and about the deer Aron's pa had seen by the sinkhole. But I didn't tell them I found the deer and couldn't kill it, because they wouldn't understand. I mean, because our world was a place of killing things: rabbits, possums, chickens, and hogs. Of course it wasn't done for fun or sport, but because it was them or us. I mean, if we wanted to live.

I seemed to be thinkin' a lot on that, lately. Grandma said the Good Book said it was okay for folks to eat meat, and I reckoned I'd give almost anything for a big platter of fried chicken right then. Instead, we had black-eyed peas and corn bread.

After we ate, I did the chores as usual, and we spent the evening in front of the fireplace shelling corn for Grandma to make hominy out of. To my way of thinking, there weren't a whole lot of things better than hot hominy with gobs of butter and salt and pepper. Of course, it took a day or more to make, what with having to soak the corn in lye water and boiling it so long, but it was worth waiting for.

I thought, sourly, that ol' Sue Ella liked to eat as well as me, except that when I ate it looked like a hog stuffin' and Sue Ella looked like she was pecking like a bird. After she'd ate every bit as much as me, folks would urge her to eat more, because they thought she hadn't hardly eaten a bite.

I told myself if I didn't quit thinking of Sue Ella I'd go plumb crazy. Seemed I'd been jealous of her all my life, maybe 'cause she had a ma and pa. It was time to admit to myself that I'd never have what she did, and maybe if I did I wouldn't want it. I'd stop thinking of her at all. I would. I would!

To get my mind off Sue Ella, I said, "Grandpa, have you knowed Homer Ragland very long?"

"Law yes, child," he said, "knowed him since he was borned, and his pa 'fore him. They's been Raglands in these hills long as we been here. Homer was ever one fer hurt things," Grandpa went on. " 'Tis a shame he didn't git to go on to school at Little Rock and become a vet doc like he wonted to be. But his

pa died, so Homer had to stay and keer fer his ma
and the little younguns. But that didn't stop him from
heppin' animals and sech. Seemed he was never without cages of squirrels with broke legs, and birds with
wings that couldn't fly. Homer do have a way with
wild things, he do."

Grandpa sighed, then added, "I've seen that man
calm down a mad bull jest talkin' to it. And they ain't
a hound dog in these hills mean enough to bite Homer
Ragland, though they'd chew somebody else's leg plumb
off."

Grandpa hushed and stared into the fire and Grandma
rocked. Shelling her lapful of corn, she said, "They
be funny folks in some ways, gal, the Raglands. Don't
eat no meat, no meat of any kind, jest make do with
what grows in their garden or what grows wild in the
woods."

"Cain't imagine a body passin' up a platter of brown
fried pork chops," Grandpa said wistfully. I sort of
agreed with him, yet on the other hand I remembered
the soft, gentle eyes of the deer and thought I was
beginning to understand Homer Ragland.

I went to bed thinking I must have dreamed that
Homer Ragland shot Tom Satterfield. The next morning Aron come over by himself to say that he and his

cousins wouldn't be able to Chritmas tree hunt 'til next week. Of course, he had to say that in front of Grandpa and Grandma, but I knew he meant body hunt, not Christmas tree hunt. Tom Satterfield's body, that is. But he said for me to be ready Sunday, for Mr. McCoy was going to hitch up the horses to their big sled and sleigh ride us all to church.

Seven

I tied my hair back with string and did the chores. The smell of boiling hominy filled the house, and Grandma was making an extra-thick pan of cornbread. The pinto beans had extra slivers of salt pork. There was a big bucket of sassafras tea sitting on the back porch to get icy cold, all to get ready for Sunday, and even when Grandma and Grandpa couldn't go to church, they still made Sunday God's day.

It was snowing again, big white feathers of it, and I turned my face to the sky, catching some on my tongue. I was no more back in the kitchen door when Grandma said, "Johnny May, let's use a couple of them eggs we been a-savin' fer Christmas and make a big bucket of snow cream. I do love that snow cream."

So does Johnny May, I thought, but said nothing. I took a two-gallon milk pail and mixed the eggs, sugar, and vanilla flavoring, then poured the cream off of the top of the milk jugs into it. Going outside, I raked the clean snow off the top of the cellar 'til the bucket was full, and mixed it with the cream. Then I put a lid on it and set it out in the snow to freeze into hardness.

I heated our old black smoothing irons on the cookstove and ironed my butter-yellow dress. After that was done, there wasn't anything else left to do but wait for Sunday morning.

I went in and laid across my bed, thinking about Aron, Scott, and Bridgette. Then I got to thinking on church, and I suddenly knew if Tom Satterfield was alive at all, he'd be at church. I mean, he always came to church—not to hear the preacher, but to look over the girls and womenfolks not yet wed. I heard he'd looked at married women when he felt like it, too.

Homer and Miz Ragland always came to church, too, so I reckoned by tomorrow we'd know for certain if Tom Satterfield was deader than a doornail or not.

While we ate supper, Grandma told Grandpa about the card from Sue Ella's ma, saying she was taking

Sue Ella to Little Rock to buy her new clothes for Christmas and maybe a gold chain for her neck. I hoped fierce she'd hang herself with it, and said sarcastically, "I bet she gets ever'thing to match her eyes."

I guess Grandpa seen the look on my face, for he said, "I allus thought yer eyes pretty, Johnny May. Sorta the color of dark maple with a tech of gold honey. Match yer hair, they do."

"And yer eyes is so big, sometimes most of yr face is eyes," Grandma added gently.

A feeling of love for the old people nigh choked me. Then I nigh ruined it all by saying, "Sue Ella has the best Christmases."

I saw Grandma clamp her lips so tight, a white line ringed her mouth, and Grandpa's eyes dulled over. I felt sick at what I'd done to them and said loud and gay as I could, "But I shore wouldn't trade my Christmas for hers. I mean, me and Aron McCoy and his cousins have had more fun looking for our Christmas tree than Christmas itself."

I seen the looks on the old people's faces loose into smiles, and knew I'd fooled them again.

"I ain't a-sayin' what all we're gonna have," I went on, " 'cause it's a secret from you, Grandpa and Grandma, but I bet ol' Sue Ella'd give her eye teeth fer a hunk of it." And deep inside a sickness rose up in me, because I knew if I got another chance I was going to kill that deer. I would kill it for Grandpa and Grandma, so's they'd have a Christmas feast to beat all.

"And the McCoys is a-comin' to our house," I said loudly, and wondered how I was going to be able to talk them into it, for old Aron was really looking forward to that fat goose. I didn't know what other lies I would have told, because Grandma broke in, talking about the sleigh ride to church.

That night I lay in my bed listening to the soft, gentle snores from the old folks' room, when something wet and heavy thudded against my window. I leaped up and went to peer out. The snow had stopped, and in the moonlight I saw Aron McCoy, ready to splash my window again.

I grabbed the window and heaved it upward, hissing, "Aron, what the devil are ye a-doin' here this time of night?"

"We sneaked out," Aron said, pointing at Scott and Bridgette over his shoulder. "Come on, Johnny May. Come and join us."

Suddenly the night come alive with excitement. "Wait! Wait for me!" I called in a loud whisper, dressing fast in the dark.

Then I was sliding through the window into the arms of a laughing Scott and Aron. There seemed to be something free about sneaking out of the house at night. I mean sorta free of trouble and troubling thoughts.

The moon was a clear pale yellow, and the stars so big they seemed to glance off the snow. Every tree looked like a Christmas tree, and we all four helt hands as we ran through the woods to a hill covered in deep snow.

We climbed the hill, sliding and laughing, rolling each other in the snow and laying on our backs to make angel wings. We threw the soft snow at each other, and at the top of the hill we found the cardboard boxes Scott and Aron had brought. Aron slit their sides with his knife and we spread them out, laying on them on our bellies, and flew down the hill on the slick snow, tumbling headfirst into a snowbank.

We sat in the snow laughing for no reason at all, and I thought that maybe I was never so happy before.

Course, I knew it was wrong to sneak out without telling our folks, but somehow it didn't seem wrong, maybe because it was so much fun to sorta have the world to ourselves.

As if Bridgette read my mind, she spread her arms

We flew down the hill on the slick snow, tumbling headfirst into a snowbank.

toward the moon, saying, "The whole world is ours, there is no one else alive but us."

"And you're nuts!" Scott laughed. "And I bet you'd run home fast enough if a big old bear came through those trees."

"Me, too," Aron said, laying back in the snow, and I said, "Let's stay here all night. Let's stay here forever."

"I think moonlight makes girls crazy," Aron said to Scott, so me and Bridgette rolled him in the snow.

Tiring of that, we decided to build a snowman, and we did a huge one without eyes or mouth and just a stick for a nose. Then, wore out, we sorta laid sleepily in the snow and talked.

Aron suddenly said, "You know, I feel closer to God here than in church."

"Me, too," I agreed. "It's almost like a body can reach up and tetch Him."

"Maybe a person could, if they could reach high enough."

"Our preacher says that God lives inside a person," Scott said, staring up at the stars, "but I think He lives up there someplace, too."

"I think God is everywhere," Aron said, real soft. "I mean, it sure felt like He was at the Brush Arbor meeting where me and Johnny May got saved."

"How come ye all sneaked out tonight?" I asked.

"We just didn't feel like going to sleep, and I sure hope Dad don't catch us coming back," Aron said hopefully.

"I hope I don't get caught, either," I said. "I don't reckon Grandma and Grandpa would understand 'not bein' able to sleep.' "

Some of the fun seemed to drain out of the night, and we walked slowly toward home.

The next morning I brushed my hair 'til it gleamed and wrapped the hateful gunnysacks around my feet. Then I heard the jingle of the harness and Aron calling, "C'mon, Johnny May!"

I climbed up on the sled and sat by Bridgette on the loose hay. Mr. McCoy slapped the horse with the reins and we were off, sliding smoothly on the hard-frozen snow. From above, the large featherlike flakes fell gentle as a baby's breath again, almost as if the moonlit night was a dream.

Suddenly Bridgette said, real loud, "Johnny May, you have the prettiest hair I ever saw, almost a red-brown, like maple leaves turning color."

Aron and Scott both turned to stare at my hair, and Aron said, "Gee whiz, Johnny May, I didn't know your hair was so long."

Scott started to reach out and touch it, but I gave a sudden squeal and said, "Catch me! I'm sliding off the straw."

Scott and Aron grabbed me, dragging me back up between them. Bridgette rolled her eyes heavenward and I slunk down, trying to fade into the straw. I bet neither Aron nor Scott would even remember to look for Tom Satterfield at church. Fact of the matter, I forgot to even tell them.

It was peaceful sliding under the trees with the jingle of the harness on the bay mare sounding happy and gay. There were already other sleds in front of the one-room school we used for a church, and a few pickups. People were laughing and calling to each other through the snow, and it was hard to see who was there or not. Once we got settled on the long benches, I looked carefully around me and especially toward the back, where the big boys stood so they could get a good look at the big girls. But Tom Satterfield wasn't there with them.

Homer and Miz Ragland were sitting on the front bench like they always did, and I stared at the kind, gentle face of Homer and never heard a word the preacher said.

Eight

I will say one thing for Aron and Scott, they did look around now and then. So did Bridgette, and I knew they were looking for Tom Satterfield. It was also a plain fact that they spent most of their time staring at girls—Aron and Scott, that is. I wished I'd have braided my hair so tight it would've pulled me bald headed. I figured nobody would notice anyways.

I did hear the preacher say that due to the weather there would be no church until it cleared up, and that might not be until spring. It was always so in our hills. No school or church because crops had to be planted or because of harvest or because it was too cold to walk the miles to the one-room school. I didn't really care so much, for I felt closer to God out in the hills and woods He had made, anyway, though Grandpa said going to church was like taking a body's car to the gas station; that church was to give a body a refill on Christian spirit, just as a gas pump filled a car to make it run for a while longer. Maybe Grandpa was right about most folks, but my refill still came from the woods and the streams, where I could plain see the beauty God made for us.

Then I thought of the deer, its big innocent eyes, the slender legs, and the way it seemed to flow over the fallen logs.

After church I caught up with Mr. McCoy while the others were lagging behind and said, "Mr. McCoy, could I ask ye a kindly favor?"

Looking down at me with eyes like Aron's, he said, "You surely can, Johnny May."

"Wal, 'tis about Christmas. You see, Grandpa and Grandma cain't git out in this weather. And Grandpa's rheumatism is acting up fierce, and they ever did like company. And I was a-wonderin' iffen you all would bring yer goose and come have Christmas with us. Not 'cause ye got a goose," I said real quick, " 'cause we'll have a bunch of good stuff cooked up. Jest come 'cause of yer company, I mean."

"Why, I think that's a grand idea, Johnny May,"

Mr. McCoy said, smiling. "In fact it would be very nice to spend the best day of the year with good neighbors."

"I shore do thank ye," I said, wringing his hand, then ran back to the others, saying loud, "Oh, Aron, you and Scott and Bridgette is a-goin' to have Christmas with us! Yer whole family, I mean. Yer ma and pa'll bring yer goose."

"And what will you have, Johnny May?"

I felt my face turn red, but said, "We're having something special, a surprise."

Then, to my surprise, Aron rubbed his belly and said to Scott and Bridgette, "Man, you haven't lived until you've eaten some of Johnny May's grandma's pinto beans. Makes me hungry just to think about them."

I grinned at Aron and then, laughing, we all ran for the sled. On the way home we were telling of Christmas tree hunting, when Mr. McCoy said, "Sorry, kids, but I need help on the farm tomorrow. You'll have to wait until the next day to go again."

I didn't say anything, but I was glad, because I had hunting of my own to do, and it wasn't for Christmas trees, either.

I went to bed feeling sad. I blew out the lamp and

was haunted through the dark night by a large pair of gentle brown eyes.

The next morning, when I came in from doing chores, Grandma peered at me, saying, "You look peaked, Johnny May, and ye hardly touched yer breakfast. Be ye ailin', gal?"

"Naw, jest wontin' some rabbit dumplin's." I grinned the best I could. I braided my hair tight, tying it with string, and wrapped my feet.

Nobody noticed I took more shells than usual, and I headed out the door toward the old sinkhole. In my pocket, under Grandpa's old coat, was our sharpest butcher knife, and it felt like it weighed a hundred pounds. It almost burdened me down in the snow.

Deep inside me was a stranger, like I wasn't Johnny May at all, but somebody who stood off watching another Johnny May. There was a lot of new snow from the overcast sky, and the drifts were deep, almost tugging the sacks off my feet in places.

The thick-growing trees seemed to slip closer and closer to me, as if they were trying to keep me out of the woods. And I knew why. When I got to the old sinkhole the deer was waiting, as if it knew I'd be there and why.

It raised its head proud, and its body quivered as

it looked straight at me with its gentle eyes. For an instant the whole woods went still and quiet, even the snow stopped spitting. My arms felt heavy, almost beyond bearing, as I lifted the gun. For a moment the deer posed to leap as if it had changed its mind about waiting for me, and the sound of the shot rang in my ears. The deer gave a tired, limping leap, then crumpled to the snow.

I took the butcher knife and knelt beside it, cutting its throat to bleed it, and as the red of its life's blood streamed across the white snow, the two Johnny Mays come together and I screamed a deep, gut-tearing, silent scream that tore my throat but made no sound.

I tried not to hear the stillness of the woods or think about the other wild things shivering in fear. Fact of the matter, I tried not to think at all as I dressed out that deer, leaving the head and entrails for the foxes and other meat-eating animals to clear up. I tied the deer's back legs with heavy twine to my empty gun and dragged it toward home, slowly, leaving a trail of blood in the snow.

Something inside me screamed *no! no! no!* over and over, denying I had killed such a beautiful live thing.

It took the rest of the day to get the deer home and into the empty shed at the back of the barn. I

I dragged it toward home, slowly, leaving a trail of blood in the snow.

knew it would freeze stiff and keep for months or until thaw, but it was a Christmas for Grandpa and Grandma. It would show folks like old Aron McCoy and his fat goose that we could have a Christmas special, too. Not that Aron bragged or anything—I was just eager to be mad at somebody. But most of all it showed me, Johnny May, that there would never, not ever, be any Christmas for me.

As I scrubbed blood from my hands with snow, a deep shame came up in me. A shame that I had killed something because of my pride, and not because of Christmas at all, and I wished fierce to have the deer living again. I would have been happy to eat pinto beans every day of the year and twice on Christmas.

On the way up to the house I had to stop and puke twice.

Nine

Grandma was putting supper on the table, and for the first time I could remember, I wasn't hungry.

Grandma said, "You git somethin' in ye, gal. Yer a-shakin' like a dog messin' peach seeds."

"I ain't hungry," I muttered. Then louder, "You all go ahead and eat, Grandma. I'll jest git the chores done and git to bed. Reckon I walked further than I aimed to."

"The gun's been shot," Grandpa said, taking it from my hands.

"I missed," I said shortly, and headed back to the barn to do the chores. All the time I was thinking of the deer hanging in the shed.

When everything was done, I poured hot water from the teakettle and washed my hands and face again. I almost fell into bed before I could get my clothes off. I pulled the covers over my ears and shut my eyes tight as I could, then let them fly wide open again, for behind my eyelids I could just see the deer's eyes and the bloody snow. When I did fall asleep it was, to my surprise, deep and dreamless.

When I woke, it was to a growling empty belly and the good smell of Grandma's biscuits. But my first thought, jumping out of bed, was that I hoped if Homer Ragland had shot Tom Satterfield, we wouldn't find out.

I mean, I hurt so bad over the deer, goose bumps rose on my body, and I started thinking how a man like Homer, who loved all animals, must feel a-hurtin' a human being. It sort of seemed like a different Johnny May got out of bed that morning. I mean, I still ate to busting, and talked real cheerful to Grandpa and Grandma so they wouldn't feel bad. But inside, I felt dead.

I did the chores and brought the big pumpkin we'd been saving for Christmas pies in from the corncrib. Grandma liked to cook pumpkin with molasses and spices and brown sugar and let it sit in a crock a few weeks before Christmas to let all the flavor soak up, she said.

The days slipped toward Christmas, almost in a dream to me. And all the time the deer, hanging cold and stiff in the shed, lived in the back of my mind. And in my dreams at night it leaped logs in the forest, its proud head held high, as it moved swift as a bird over the snow.

Fact of the matter, I thought maybe I'd never feel nothing ever again. When Sue Ella's folks came and brought us some oranges and apples for Christmas, Grandma said, "Law, law, Johnny May, we got us the fixin's of pumpkin pies, but I do reckon 'tis all we can add to the company feast."

"Now, you jest don't worry on no feast, Grandma," I said. "We done got our share to add. I ain't a-tellin' ye 'til Christmas Eve, 'cause 'tis yer and Grandpa's present from me."

Aron, Scott, and Bridgette came over and we looked for trees, and I mean really looked for trees, because no matter what Aron said, I wouldn't look for Tom Satterfield's body anymore.

He glared at me angrily, saying, "Don't you care, Johnny May? Don't you care that a man might have been murdered?"

"Yes, I do," I said stubbornly, "but you know well as me Homer is a good man, and I don't wont him hurt none."

"Well, he don't seem all that good to me if he killed someone," Aron said, but hushed after he saw that I wasn't going to change my mind.

A week before Christmas, Aron, Scott, and Bridgette spent the night with me, and they laughed and ate up a whole pot of beans and a pan of cornbread, and didn't seem to mind at all.

We stayed up late popping corn and stringing it for our tree, one that nigh reached the ceiling. And while we strang and ate popcorn, Grandpa and Grandma cracked walnuts and picked out the meat with horseshoe nails so we could make a big batch of molasses candy for Christmas.

For the first time since I killed the deer, I felt almost happy, at least I felt something for a change. We tied strings around the oranges and apples and hung them from the tree, and their smell mingled with the scent of pine and made the whole house look and smell like Christmas.

The next morning we made so much candy, there was plenty to send home with the McCoys, everybody laughing and calling, "See ye at Christmas."

I dug the pickles and pear preserves out of the empty apple barrel in the barn and gave them to Grandma for the big dinner that was coming, and our house started to smell of cinnamon as Grandma baked the pumpkin pies.

On the outside of me it was nice, a Christmas feel. But inside I felt bad, real bad. On Christmas Eve the sun was shining, and the ice shone like glass all sparkly and clean. The snow was almost blinding white. At breakfast I said, "Now Grandpa, you jest stay here with Grandma at the table 'till I git the chores done, then I'm bringin' in yer Christmas present."

I hurried through the chores, then pulled the deer down from the rafters of the shed where I'd hung it. I reckon it weighed more than a hundred pounds as I dragged it through the snow to the house.

I opened the back door, heaving to lift the deer, and heard Grandpa gasp, "Lordy mercy, Ma, Johnny May done killed our cow!"

"It ain't no cow, Grandpa," I said, heaving the deer the rest of the way into the kitchen. "It's a deer, a deer for you and Grandma's Christmas. I killed it a couple of weeks ago," I said, straightening up and watching the looks on their faces, Grandpa squinting his eyes admiringly at it, and Grandma walking around it saying, "Oh, law, law, what a feast we'll have! Why, they's enough meat there to have steaks and roast and stew and venison chili. Why, Pa, they's most enough meat here to last 'til spring garden truck comes in. And Johnny May, gal, ye couldn'ta got me and yer Grandpa nothin' we'd like better."

I grinned big as I could at them and fled to my room, flinging myself down on the bed and closing my eyes tight. I didn't know how long I laid there, but after a while I could smell meat cooking, and I knew Grandpa and Grandma would stay up all night cooking for the company coming.

They were happy. I could hear them laughing and Grandma saying, "Hand me them onions, Pa," or "We best grind up some red pepper." I knew I ought to have felt happy because they were, but I couldn't.

It wasn't 'til after chore time that it hit me what I had to do. After a supper of beans, I said, "Grandpa, can I go walkin' a little? 'Cause the moon's shinin' so pretty on the snow."

"Why, I reckon, gal, and iffen I was younger I'd go with ye."

"Ye wrap up good, gal," Grandma said. " 'Tis colder than cold when the sky is clear."

I put on my old coat, wrapped my feet, and stepped out into the cold, crisp night air. Grandpa and Grandma didn't know it, but I was going to look for me a Christmas of my own.

Ten

The moon and the stars hung low and bright in the still, white night. The sky looked deep, a blue-black. The Milky Way and the Big and Little Dippers were plain to see. Snow crunched with a crisp snap under my feet and I peered at the deep darkness under the trees. My ears and nose stung from the cold air, and my breath hung before my face in white puffs.

My strides were long and steady, my feet eating up the miles as I thought that surely the large star just ahead of me must be the very one that led the wise men to the Christ child, but it was leading me to a wise man. I prayed to myself: *Please, Lord, let him be a wise man.*

When I knocked on the door, Miz Ragland looked surprised and said, "Why, Johnny May. Ye git a hurtin' cow or somethin'?"

I nodded and she laughed gently, saying, "Wal, ye know where to find Homer."

I nodded again and went around the house to the barn. Yellow light, warm colored, spilled from the open barn door and the cracks around the building, between the boards. When I walked inside, it felt warm and smelled of new milk and the sunshine still trapped in the clean straw on the floor and in the stalls. And it also smelled of something soft and new-born.

Homer was sitting on a bale of hay under a lantern hanging from the ceiling, holding the tiny calf we had seen before in his arms.

He looked up at me, a gentle look still in his large, dark eyes, and I dropped to the straw at his feet.

Silently he rose and put the calf in the stall with its mother, and dropping onto the hay bale again, he said, kindly, "Got a critter a-hurtin' Johnny May?"

I nodded and said brokenly, "Yes sir, Mr. Ragland, I do, and that critter is me. I'm a-hurtin' powerful bad."

"Where ye be hurt, child?" he asked, laying a hand softly on my head.

" 'Tis in here, Mister," I said, pointing to my chest, "and Mr. Ragland, 'tis a hurt hard to git at."

And without me knowing I was going to cry, sobs rose up in me harsh and sore, and I knelt weeping, spilling out how I'd seen him shoot Tom Satterfield, and about the deer and the blood in the snow, and the innocent eyes. I told him about wanting a Christmas for Grandpa and Grandma, and hating the way I'd got it for them, and how mostly I reckoned it was my pride more than anything else that made me kill the deer.

Homer let me pour it all out, and I shuddered to a stop, saying, "I reckon you might wont to kill me, too, I mean 'cause I know about Tom Satterfield. But I don't much keer, 'cause I have felt like dyin' ever since I killed that deer, anyways."

There was silence in the barn for a long spell, then Homer took my tear-stained face in his hands and slowly raised it to meet his eyes, and he said, ever so gently, "Ye pore youngun. I ain't gonna hurt ye none, not a hair on yer head. 'Tis true, I did shoot Tom Satterfield, but jest a little in the arm so's he'd know how things hurt. Ye see, child, Tom was settin' traps all over the woods, and they was times he'd let the pore critters lay fer days, their legs broke and them

Homer took my tear-stained face in his hands.

a-sufferin', 'fore he'd go see iffen they was anything in the traps. Sometimes, youngun, folks jest won't listen, so they have to be showed. Tom's all right. Fact of the matter, I took him to a town doctor. 'Twas jest a scratch, but Tom decided to try city livin' fer a spell.

"Now, Johnny May, as fer you a-killin' that deer, 'tis no sin, I reckon, 'cause the Good Book says folks can eat meat. Fact, it says what God has cleaned, let no man call unclean. But fer as I know, God didn't say ye *had* to eat it, neither. Me and mine choose not to, but I'll tell ye this, iffen we was hungry, I'd kill us a deer or somethin'. Ye understand, child?"

I nodded, saying, "Ye mean you'd rather not kill things to eat, but iffen you was pore you would?"

Homer nodded, and I said with a deep sigh, "We was pore, real pore. Jest beans and more beans. Every blessed day, beans."

"Wal, then, they ain't no need of you a-frettin', is there now?" Homer said.

I rose to my feet, saying, "No, they ain't, and I shorely do thank ye, Mister, fer this here talk."

"Why, yer real welcome, Johnny May," Homer said. Then he added softly, "Ye know, 'tis nigh Christmas day. Close on to midnight. I've allus heerd that at midnight on Christmas Eve, the animals all kneel down in honor of the birthin' of Christ, our Lord. Would you like to stay and see iffen it be true, Johnny May?"

"That I would, Mister," I said sincerely, "but I best git a-runnin' home, least Grandpa'll come lookin' fer me." And calling, "Merry Christmas to you and yours," I ran out the barn door toward home.

As I ran I thought of tomorrow and the McCoys, of Scott and Bridgette, of being together in a house that smelled of spices, baking meat, and the sound of laughter. For a moment I turned my head and looked at the bright star that seemed to hang over Homer Ragland's place, and I smiled up at it, thinking tomorrow I'd tell Scott and Aron and Bridgette that Homer hadn't killed anyone.

Then, laughing for no reason at all, I ran on toward home, sending snow flying under my feet. Old Aron was going to have help eating his goose. I was real glad now that I had given Grandpa and Grandma a Christmas, but I didn't have to eat any of it. Fact of the matter, my Christmas was inside me, dancing and happy to beat all.

About the Author

ROBBIE BRANSCUM has written numerous books for young people, including another book about this spunky young girl, called simply JOHNNY MAY. Her most recent book, THE MURDER OF HOUND DOG BATES, was honored with an Edgar for Best Juvenile Mystery.

Like Johnny May, Ms. Branscum grew up in the Arkansas Hills, where she attended a one-room schoolhouse until the seventh grade. She completed her education on her own in the public libraries, and writes to "give other people the joy that books gave me."

She now lives on a small farm in Eufaula, Oklahoma, where she raises calves, chickens, and vegetables, and, of course, writes.

About the Artist

DEBORAH HOWLAND has illustrated a number of children's books, the first of which was THE SCARED ONE. She studied at the School of Visual Arts in New York City. Ms. Howland now lives in Weston, Connecticut, with her husband and three children.